THE PUPPY PLACE

ROXY

THE PUPPY PLACE

Don't miss any of these
other stories by Ellen Miles!

THE PUPPY PLACE

ROXY

ELLEN MILES

SCHOLASTIC INC.

Copyright © 2019 by Ellen Miles
Cover art by Tim O'Brien
Original cover design by Steve Scott

All rights reserved. Published by Scholastic Inc., *Publishers since 1920.* SCHOLASTIC and associated logos are trademarks and/or registered trademarks of Scholastic Inc.

This book is a work of fiction. Names, characters, places, and incidents are either the product of the author's imagination or are used fictitiously, and any resemblance to actual persons, living or dead, business establishments, events, or locales is entirely coincidental.

ISBN 978-1-338-30306-3

10 9 8 7 6 5 4 3 2 1   19 20 21 22 23

Printed in the U.S.A.   40
First printing 2019

CHAPTER ONE

"Did you see the girl who was explaining her experiment on how mushrooms can save the planet?" Sammy asked. "That was so cool."

Charles nodded. "She made a whole movie about it and everything." He sighed. "I don't think our science fair projects are going to come anywhere close to that," he said.

Sammy shrugged. "Well, we're only in second grade," he said with a grin. "That girl was a senior in high school."

"Exactly," said Charles's dad, from the driver's seat. He met Charles's eyes in the mirror. "When you're a high school senior, you can invent some new way for people to communicate or fly into space. But for now, I'm sure Mr. Mason will be happy with—I don't know—maybe a project on raising tadpoles."

Charles and Sammy cracked up. "No, he won't!" said Sammy. "He made a rule this year: no tadpoles."

"He said he'll be happy if he never sees another tadpole again," Charles added. "He said he's had six years of tadpoles and that's enough." Mr. Mason was always saying funny things. He was the best teacher ever, and Charles really wanted to make him proud by doing a great project for the Littleton Elementary School science fair. That's why he and his best friend, Sammy, had convinced Charles's dad to take them to the high school science fair that night after dinner. They'd been hoping to find some inspiration at the fair, but instead, Charles just felt overwhelmed. All the projects were so impressive.

"Did you see that robot?" he asked Sammy. "The one that could shoot a basketball into a hoop? I think the guy who built it is only a freshman."

"Everybody's doing robots lately," Sammy said, shrugging. "I heard Jason is building a robot for our science fair."

"Yeah, from a kit his dad bought for him," said Charles. "All that shows is that he can follow directions. That guy tonight invented his whole robot from scratch! I heard he's going to enter it in a national robotics competition."

"Robot, bobot, dobot," sang the Bean from his car seat. "Beep, beep, beep!"

"That's right!" said Charles, holding up a hand to give his little brother a high five. "Robots say beep-beep."

"Boop-boop," said the Bean, laughing his gurgly laugh. "Goop-goop. Zeep-zeep."

Charles and Sammy cracked up again. Charles was glad Dad had decided to bring the Bean along, even if it meant that they'd had to walk very slowly through the science fair. It was always fun to go places with the Bean, because everyone loved him. He got a lot of attention. It was sort of like having a cute puppy along.

"Lizzie would have liked that exhibit on how to measure dog intelligence," said Charles. His older sister was a total dog expert. "She would have been impressed by the border collie who knew over two hundred words."

"I think I'm glad that Buddy isn't quite that smart," said Dad. "Your aunt Amanda always says that dogs who are too smart can be trouble."

Charles laughed. He was thankful that Buddy had been smart enough, and cute enough, and charming enough, to make the whole Peterson family fall in love with him when he first came to them as a foster puppy. Unlike all the other puppies they had fostered, who had only stayed a short time, Buddy had stayed forever, becoming part of the family.

Sometimes Charles still couldn't believe how lucky he was that he and Lizzie had convinced their parents to be a foster family. He loved getting to know each of the dogs they took care of, and making sure that each one went to the perfect home. It was always sad to say good-bye when it was time to let them go, but having Buddy made it easier. With Buddy in the house, there was always a puppy to play with, to tell secrets to, and to cuddle with under the covers at night.

"I'm thinking mold," Sammy announced just then.

Charles turned to stare at his friend. "Mold?" he asked.

"Sure," said Sammy. "I mean, for my science fair project. What could be easier or more fun? I heard about a third grader who did it last year. You take a bunch of different foods and liquids and leave them sealed up in plastic bags on the counter for a week or so, just to find out what grows on them. Some things grow green or yellow mold, some grow long white hairy stuff, and some just get all jellified and gross." He grinned.

"I'm sure your mom will love that," said Charles's dad. He stopped at a red light and turned to smile at the boys.

"She will," said Sammy. "She's really into science. I bet she'll get her microscope out. She'll probably try to identify every mold. It's my dad who won't like it. He's totally creeped out by moldy

6

stuff. He's always throwing leftovers out, even before they get old."

"Uppy!" said the Bean, who had been staring out the window.

"That's right, we'll see Buddy soon," Charles said. He knew that "uppy" was sometimes the Bean's way of saying "puppy." "We're almost home."

The Bean shook his head. "Uppy!" he said again. He pointed. "Uppy-uppy-uppy!"

Charles leaned over to look, wondering what his little brother was talking about. It was getting dark out, and at first, he didn't see anything. Then he spotted a tiny white fluff ball, sitting very still in the tall grass on the side of the road. "Dad!" he said. "Pull over! The Bean is right. It's a puppy!"

CHAPTER TWO

"What?" Dad asked. "A puppy?"

"Yes!" said Charles. "And I think she's hurt."
He watched as the little fluff ball tried to stand.
She struggled to her feet, then sat down with one
paw up, staring back at Charles with a pleading
expression.

Help me, please! I'm all alone.

"Dad!" Charles urged again. "We have to help!"
As soon as the light turned green, Dad took a
right turn and pulled the van over. He unbuckled

his seat belt and was out of the van before Charles could say another word. Charles and Sammy unbuckled, too. Charles started to get out, but Dad turned around and held up a hand. "Uh-uh, hold on there. I want you two to stay in the van with the Bean."

"But—" Charles began.

Dad headed toward the puppy. Charles saw him squat down and reach out gently. "Oh, please be okay," Charles whispered. "Please be okay, little puppy."

"What's a puppy that young doing out here all by herself?" Sammy asked. "Poor thing."

The boys watched as Charles's dad stood up again, cradling something white and fluffy in his arms. Charles pulled off his sweatshirt. "She'll need a soft place to lie down," he said. He folded up the sweatshirt and put it over his knees.

Dad walked up to the van and nodded at Charles to open the door. He leaned over to place the puppy on Charles's lap. "Be very gentle," he said. "I think she might have a broken leg."

Charles looked at the puppy's front legs and saw that she was still holding one of them up as if it hurt—a lot. He felt his stomach tighten. Very carefully, he stroked the dog's head with one finger. "You're going to be okay," he whispered.

Dad pulled out his phone. "I'm going to call Dr. Gibson," he said. Dr. Gibson was the Petersons' vet. She was always ready to help with their foster puppies.

"See?" Charles said to the puppy. "We're going to help you." The puppy snuggled into the sweatshirt on Charles's lap and looked up at him with her big brown eyes.

I know you're going to take care of me. I trust you.

Charles could tell that this puppy was one tough little girl. She didn't even whimper as she held up her hurt paw.

She was so cute Charles could hardly resist giving her a huge hug, but he held back. He didn't want to hurt her leg. Her funny, furry face was white, and her floppy ears were brown. The rest of her coat was spotted brown and white, and her little tail was all brown with a white spot on the very tip. She was smaller than Buddy, but she looked like a sturdy little thing. Charles could tell that if her leg wasn't hurting, this wiry pup would probably be able to run circles around Buddy.

"Hi, Dr. Gibson?" Dad said into his phone. "I know it's after hours, but I've got a favor to ask—" He stopped short. "Oh, you are?" He paused. "You do? Well—okay, then. I guess we'll see you in a few minutes."

He touched the screen to hang up and sat staring at the phone in his hand for a moment.

"Dad?" Charles said. "Let's get going. This puppy really needs some help." Even though the puppy was such a brave little thing, he knew she must be hurting. He remembered when he'd broken his ankle, falling off the old swing set in the backyard. It had been painful. Really, really painful.

Dad nodded and started the van.

"What did the vet say?" Sammy asked.

"That's the funny thing," Dad said. "Dr. Gibson is at her office, even though it's after closing time. She didn't sound surprised at all to hear from me—and she said she had a surprise for us."

"Weird," said Sammy. He reached over to stroke the little pup's face with one gentle finger.

Charles wasn't really paying attention to the conversation. All he'd heard was that Dr. Gibson was waiting for them. "Come on, Dad, let's go!" he urged. He could feel the puppy's small warm body trembling a bit.

"We're on our way," said Dad, pulling out onto the road.

Charles wished Dad could put on a siren, the way he did when he drove the fire truck during an emergency. A vehicle with a siren and lights was allowed to go really fast and run through red lights. The sooner they got to Dr. Gibson's the better.

Even without the siren, it didn't take long. Soon, they were pulling into the vet's parking lot. Charles unbuckled as soon as the van came to a stop, and leapt out with the puppy in his arms.

"Easy, kiddo," said his dad. "Careful with that precious cargo."

Charles slowed down and climbed carefully up the stairs to the vet's front door. Dr. Gibson opened the door the moment he stepped onto the porch. "Come in!" she said. "We've been waiting for you."

Charles heard a whimper and then loud whining from behind Dr. Gibson. The little pup in his arms let out an answering cry as she squirmed and wriggled, trying to get down.

The vet stepped aside so Charles could see into the large dog crate in front of the reception desk.

Charles stared. "Whoa!" he said.

CHAPTER THREE

Charles peered into the crate. Staring back at him was a dog who looked a whole lot like the puppy in his arms, only twice as big. She lay curled up on a comfy bed, and tucked in with her were two small puppies who were nearly identical to the one Charles held.

Charles looked at Dr. Gibson. "Is that—"

The vet seemed to read his mind. She nodded before he even finished his sentence. "I think so, don't you?"

"That's her mom? And her brothers—or sisters?" Charles didn't really have to ask. He could tell by the looks of the dog and her puppies, and by the way the mother dog whimpered and whined. As he watched, she stood up and pawed at the side of the crate, whining even more loudly.

"Seems like it's time for a family reunion," said Dr. Gibson. "Your pup looks just like her mom and two brothers. I think they're all some kind of mix, maybe Cavalier King Charles spaniel and—I don't know what. Chihuahua, maybe?"

The puppy in his arms squirmed harder. "Can they say hi?" Charles asked.

"Of course," said Dr. Gibson. She went to open the crate. "The mom has been absolutely wild ever since she was dropped off here, an hour ago. I had to put her in the crate, because if she was free, she tried to run out the door every five seconds. I had a feeling she might be missing one of her pups."

The dog flashed out of the crate, a brown-and-white blur heading straight for Charles. Quickly, he knelt down, holding the little puppy firmly so she wouldn't jump out of his arms and hurt her leg. The mother dog gently nuzzled and licked the puppy's face, as if she knew her pup was hurt. The little puppy couldn't stop whimpering with joy.

Mom! Mom! I'm so happy to see you!

The sound made Charles's heart melt. It was obvious how excited the two dogs were to see each other.

Now the other two puppies came tumbling out of the crate. They ran, scrabbling across the slippery floor, to see their sister. Again, the puppy in Charles's arms began to squirm and whine, but Charles held her snugly. "Her leg is hurt," he told Dr. Gibson. "I don't want to let her down."

"Good idea," said the vet. "Let's bring the whole family back to the exam room and I'll take a look at her."

No leashes or collars were necessary. Charles and his dad and the Bean and Sammy followed Dr. Gibson, and the mother dog and two puppies followed close behind them. It was quite a parade. The puppies scampered clumsily across the floor while the mother dog pranced along delicately, staring up at the third puppy in Charles's arms.

"This one must be a little adventurer," said Dr. Gibson as she took the puppy from Charles and set her on the high exam table. "The guy who brought in the rest of the family said he thought he might have seen one puppy running off. He decided it was most important to save the mom, since she and her family were right on the side of the road."

"I wonder how she got hurt," Dad said. "Do you think she might have been hit by a car?"

"Anything's possible," said Dr. Gibson. "Stray dogs have a tough life, especially young puppies. And at this age, her bones are very fragile and could break easily." She put her stethoscope to the puppy's chest and listened carefully, then began to touch her gently all over. When she touched the hurt leg, the puppy let out a tiny squeal.

Charles saw the mother's ears stand up. She whined softly, as if to say, *Be strong, little one.*

Dr. Gibson felt the leg carefully, watching the pup's face closely. "It may only be a sprain and not a broken bone," she said finally, "but the only way to know is to do an X-ray. That will also help me be sure that nothing else is wrong. Can you all watch the rest of the family while I do that?"

Charles nodded. "Of course," he said.

He watched as Dr. Gibson lifted the puppy off the table and headed to a back room. The puppy's mom watched, too—but Charles noticed that she didn't whimper. "I think she's happy to know that her puppy is safe," Charles said.

"Definitely," Dad agreed. "She doesn't seem as upset anymore, now that she's seen her little girl."

Sammy was holding one of the pups. He stroked his tiny head and murmured softly into his ear. "You're safe, too," he said. "You've had some big adventures, but you're safe now."

Dad held the other puppy, while Charles stroked the mother dog's side, trying to keep her calm. "What do you think they were doing on the side of the road, anyway?" Charles asked his dad.

Dad shook his head, frowning. "Maybe the mom was a runaway, but I have a feeling she's a stray, with no home. She isn't wearing a collar, and look at how you can see her ribs sticking out.

The poor thing hasn't had a decent meal in a long time."

Charles nodded. The mother dog was very skinny. Her fur was matted in places, and she had a scratch on her face. "You've had a tough life," he said to her. "But maybe things will get better now."

Dr. Gibson came back into the room, cradling the puppy. "Good news," she said. "I don't see any broken bones or other problems, so it's probably just a sprain. She'll need some time to heal, but she won't need surgery, or even a cast." She set the puppy down on the exam table and reached for supplies from a cabinet beneath it.

The mother dog gazed up at the puppy but still did not whine. She wagged her little tail as she watched Dr. Gibson wrap the puppy's leg in purple tape.

"Now what?" Charles asked when she was done. "Is the whole family going to stay here tonight?"

He knew there were cages in the back, where dogs could spend the night if they were really sick or had just had an operation.

Dr. Gibson opened her mouth to answer, but just then, someone *yoo-hoo*ed from the reception area.

Charles laughed. He recognized that voice. "I should have known," he said. "You already called Ms. Dobbins."

CHAPTER FOUR

"I came as soon as I could," said Ms. Dobbins as she bustled into the exam room. "Oh! I thought you said there were only two puppies." She looked at the puppies, then stared in turn at Charles, the Bean, Sammy, and Mr. Peterson. "And how did you all end up here?" She looked bewildered.

Charles's dad laughed. "You know how it is. Puppies just seem to have a way of finding us," he said. He explained about how they had picked up the puppy from the side of the road and brought her straight to Dr. Gibson.

Ms. Dobbins nodded. "Good for you." She approached the puppy on the table and gently held out a finger for her to sniff. Then she turned to Dr. Gibson. "How badly is she hurt?"

Dr. Gibson smiled. "Thankfully, the leg doesn't seem to be broken. This little girl has good luck."

"Hmm," said Ms. Dobbins. "If you consider it good luck to be born on the side of the road." She shook her head. "We see this way too often at the shelter—a stray dog with puppies. I guess the ones we find really are the lucky ones."

Charles remembered when his puppy, Buddy, had arrived at Caring Paws, along with his mom and two sisters. "Like Buddy's family," he said.

"That's right," said Ms. Dobbins. She knelt to pet the mother dog. "Hey there, darling," she said. "You've done a great job with these pups. Now you're all safe." She picked up each of the pups and examined them. "Eyes are open, teeth are in—looks like they're about eight weeks old, and starting to eat solid food. That's the perfect age for them to leave their mom and go to new homes." She turned to Dad and raised her eyebrows.

"Oh, no," he said, holding up his hands. "We can't take on three puppies. We've done it before, but it's a lot of work, and Betsy's in the middle of researching a big story right now." Charles's mom was a newspaper reporter.

Ms. Dobbins barely blinked. "How about one puppy, then?" she asked, gesturing to the puppy on the exam table.

Charles grinned. "Yes!" he whispered to Sammy, pumping his fist. Up until that moment, he had not even thought about whether his family would foster the puppy with the hurt leg. Everything had moved so fast, from the very first moment when the Bean had spotted her on the side of the road. Now, suddenly, he wanted—more than anything!—to bring this sweet puppy home and take care of her.

Dad just laughed.

"I'm serious," said Ms. Dobbins.

Dad's face changed. He stopped laughing. "Oh," he said. "Well . . ."

"I'm already full at the shelter, but I'm squeezing this mom and two pups in," said Ms. Dobbins. "We are way too busy at Caring Paws to also be caring for a pup who needs special attention."

Dr. Gibson nodded. "This puppy will need to be kept quiet for at least a few days. No running around. She needs to rest, ideally in a very calm environment."

Dad laughed again. "Well, I can't exactly say that our home is a very calm environment, with three kids and a puppy—but I suppose it's calmer than the shelter."

"She can stay in my room," said Charles. "I'll make her a cozy little bed with soft blankets and

26

towels in a big cardboard box. I'll bring her food and water and sleep right there next to her at night."

"You'll probably even read to her," Sammy said. "The way you always read the Sunday comics to Buddy."

"Awww, do you do that?" Dr. Gibson asked Charles. "That is so sweet. I bet Buddy loves that."

Charles felt himself blushing. "I guess," he said. "Anyway, we'll take really good care of her, I promise!"

"Hold on there, mister," said his dad. "I can't remember agreeing to this. Did we even talk about it?"

Charles just looked at his dad. He tried to make his eyes look as huge and pleading as Buddy's did when he was begging for a treat. If Charles had a tail, he would have wagged it. How could Dad be able to resist helping this feisty little pup? After all, that was what a foster family did. That's what the Peterson family did. They helped puppies who needed them.

Dad asked again. "Did we?"

Charles did the big-eye thing again, cocking his head this time. If he could have stuck out his ears hopefully, the way Buddy did when you asked if he wanted to go for a walk, he would have.

Dad raised his hands. "I surrender!" But then he reached for his phone and punched a button. "But only if Mom agrees."

"Yesss," Charles whispered to Sammy, with another fist pump. He knew Mom would not say no when she heard that this puppy especially needed their help.

"I knew it," Charles told Lizzie later, as they sat on the floor in his room with the brown-and-white

28

puppy. "Once I used the 'begging puppy' face on Dad, it was all over."

She held up a palm for a high five. "Well done," she said. "And this little one here did her part, too," she added, gently petting the puppy who lay nestled in Charles's old red-plaid baby blanket. Her purple-wrapped leg stuck out straight, but she looked cozy and happy. Charles could tell she enjoyed the attention.

Wait till you see me when I can run around again! Then you'll really be impressed.

"She's a little toughie," said Charles. "She made it, even out there on her own. You can tell her leg hurts, but she barely ever cries."

"I wonder if she misses her family," said Lizzie.

"That's why I put so many of Buddy's toys in with her," said Charles. "So she wouldn't feel too lonely." The puppy was surrounded by a floppy duck, a long purple snake, three cushy balls, and a mostly shredded yellow teddy bear. Looking up at Charles, she put a paw on the duck and gave her tiny head a shake.

I'll never be lonely as long as you're my friend!

CHAPTER FIVE

"Wow, that was so much fun," Sammy said to Charles. It was a few days after the Great Puppy Rescue, and they were at the snack bar at LazerQuest, eating french fries after a wild game of laser tag.

"I know," said Charles. "I hated to leave the puppy, but I couldn't miss your birthday party. Anyway, Lizzie's taking good care of her."

Another boy came over and smacked Sammy's hand. "Great shot," he said. "I thought I had you cornered in that purple room, but you escaped. Then you got me when I came through the yellow hallway."

Sammy and Charles laughed. "We ambushed so many people in that hallway," said Charles. "Green team rules!" Charles's heart was still thudding from all the crazy running around. The lights were so bright, and the music was so loud. It was like being inside a video game. *Hmm, video games.* Charles glanced over to the arcade area. "Do you have any quarters?" he asked Sammy. They had time for a few games before cake and presents.

Sammy shook his head.

"I think I could loan you a couple," said someone behind Charles. He turned to see who had spoken. It was Mr. Mason! His teacher put his soda down next to his own basket of fries and started rummaging in his pocket, looking for quarters.

"What are you doing here?" Charles asked, without even thinking. Then he felt bad. "I mean—it's funny to see you here."

32

Mr. Mason smiled. "It's funny to see you, too," he said. He put his arm around the woman standing next to him. She was pretty, with long wavy brown hair and big brown eyes that matched her brown skin. "I'm here with my sweetie. This is Janice."

Janice smiled at Charles and Sammy. "You must be in Tom's class," she said. "I mean—Mr. Mason's."

Charles and Sammy nodded. Charles was still getting used to the idea of seeing his teacher at LazerQuest. Now he also had to get used to the idea that his teacher had a first name—and a girlfriend! He stared at Mr. Mason and Janice, but somehow he couldn't think of a thing to say.

Mr. Mason seemed to understand. "How's that puppy?" he asked. Charles always told his classmates about the puppies they were fostering, and he'd already shared a lot about the new puppy.

Charles smiled. "She's doing great," he said. "She's so smart! Lizzie and I taught her some tricks already, even though her leg is hurt. She can sit up pretty and play dead."

"The puppy gets around really well on three legs, too," said Sammy. He had come over to play with the puppy that morning.

"I heard that you foster puppies," Janice said to Charles. "My son, Derek, wants to do that, too—but I'm so busy as a single mom. I work long hours as a nurse. But Derek lives with his dad three nights a week, and he might agree to fostering. They've been visiting a mother dog and two puppies over at that shelter. Caring Paws, I think it's called?"

"That's our puppy's mom!" Charles burst out. "And her brothers!" For a second, Charles wasn't sure how he felt about another family in town fostering puppies. Would there be enough to go around? He shook his head. That was silly. Of course there would. Sadly, there were always puppies who needed help. And how great would it be if someone fostered the mother dog and her puppies?

"Cool," said Janice. "That's my son over there." She pointed to some boys playing video games in the arcade. "He's here for a birthday party."

"It's my birthday, too," said Sammy.

"Oh, happy birthday!" said Janice.

Charles recognized a teenage boy from the science fair the other night—the one who had made the robot. He was tall and skinny, with an Afro and oversized glasses. He could see a resemblance to Janice—their faces were the same shape. Was that him?

"What's your puppy's name?" Janice asked. "I hear she's really cute and feisty."

Charles nodded. "She is," he said. "She doesn't have a name yet. I mean, she has a lot of names, because everybody in the family calls her something different. But nothing has stuck so far."

Janice laughed. "What are some of the names?"

"My dad calls her Rosie," said Charles, "because she's such a happy girl. And my mom calls her Moxie because she's a little toughie. Mom says that's a name for someone with a lot of spirit."

Mr. Mason nodded and popped a french fry into his mouth. "What about you? What do you call her?"

"I just call her all kinds of nicknames," said Charles. "Like Little Girl and Honey Bun. Lizzie, my sister, calls her Isabella de la Luna. I have no idea why."

"And the Bean calls her Uppy, of course," added Sammy.

Janice closed her eyes for a moment. "I'm good at naming things," she said. "Let me think. . . . How about Roxy? It's cute, and it combines Rosie and Moxie."

Charles raised his eyebrows. "Wow, that's great!" he said. Mr. Mason's girlfriend was really smart. "I bet everyone can agree on that one."

"Boys!" called Sammy's dad just then. "Time for cake and presents!" He waved from the long table he and Sammy's mom had been busy setting up.

"Have fun," said Mr. Mason.

"I hope I get to meet that puppy someday, whatever you decide to name her," said Janice, smiling at Charles. "She sounds like one special pup."

"See you two at school tomorrow," said Mr. Mason. "I can't wait to hear what you've come up with for your science fair projects." He and Janice walked off, hand in hand.

Charles's stomach fell. He stared at Sammy. "Uh-oh," he said. He had totally forgotten that Monday was the day they were supposed to tell Mr. Mason what projects they'd decided to do for the science fair.

CHAPTER SIX

"Roxy!" Lizzie said when Charles told her about the name that Janice had suggested. "Hmm, Roxy."

He held his breath. Would she like it? He looked down at the puppy in his arms. He had scooped her up the second he walked into the house, after Sammy's birthday party. She was so irresistibly cute! He kissed the top of her head, and she licked his cheek with gusto. After a few days of rest, her sore leg barely seemed to bother her. They would be taking her to see Dr. Gibson again soon, and Charles had a feeling the vet would say that the puppy was all better.

"I love it!" said Lizzie. She grinned at Charles. "It's much better than Isabella de la Luna. That name really never fit her." She reached out to stroke the puppy's tiny head. "Hi, Roxy," she said.

"Woxy!" yelled the Bean when he heard. His smile lit up his whole face.

Mom and Dad liked the name, too. "Works for me," said Dad.

"It's perfect," said Mom. "But don't forget, whoever adopts her may decide to change it."

Charles frowned. Why did she have to remind him about that? He didn't even want to think about someone adopting this puppy. That was the worst part of fostering—when you had to say good-bye. It helped when you knew you had found a puppy the perfect home, but it was still never easy. And what was the perfect home for Roxy? He looked down at the puppy in his arms. She gazed back at him from under the long, bushy eyebrows that made her face so silly and cute.

"Who's the cutest?" Charles asked.

She tilted her head and stuck her ears out in the most adorable way.

I am, silly!

The whole family burst into laughter.

"That's it!" said Lizzie. "That's Roxy's new trick! I've been trying to think of tricks I can teach a dog with a hurt leg. I'll teach her to tilt her head like that when you ask her 'Who's the cutest?'"

Hearing the phrase, Roxy tilted her head again, this time in the other direction. Her brown eyes sparkled as she held up one paw.

I told you! It's me!

"I don't think you even have to teach her," said Dad, laughing again. "She's a natural—and she knows exactly how cute she is."

"That's why it's the perfect trick," said Lizzie. "When you can take something that a dog does naturally and then reward them for it—especially with really good treats, like Aunt Amanda always uses—they learn super fast."

On Monday morning at Sharing Circle, Charles told his class about Roxy's new name and new trick. "And Janice, Mr. Mason's girlfriend, was the one who thought of the perfect name," he added.

At the word "girlfriend," everybody hooted. Mr. Mason turned bright red. "Um, thank you, Charles," he said. "Does anybody else have something to share?"

After Sharing Circle, Mr. Mason said he was going to meet with each of them individually to talk about their science fair projects. "The rest of you can do free reading, or begin work on whatever project you've chosen," he said. He sat down at his desk and called Tiffany Alexander's name.

Good, thought Charles. *He's going alphabetically. That gives me a little time.*

Charles sat at his desk, doodling pictures of cartoon dogs while he tried to think of a science fair project. Should he do mold, like Sammy? No, that was copying. How about something on plastic pollution in the ocean? He had heard Mom talking about that. Or maybe he should try growing some bean plants under different conditions? Lizzie had done that once. Charles smiled to himself, remembering how the ones she had watered with raspberry drink mix had grown more than the ones she had watered with milk.

Then he shook his head. None of those ideas really grabbed him. He thought about what

Mr. Mason had taught them about how scientists work. "Everything begins with 'I wonder,'" Mr. Mason had said. "Like, I wonder what will happen if I mix these two chemicals. Or, I wonder how birds know when it's time to fly south. I wonder if there is a way to create a whole new kind of rocket." Mr. Mason had told them to let their minds wander and to write down the things they wondered about. "You never know where that will lead," he'd said.

"Charles?" Mr. Mason called just then.

Charles gulped. It was his turn, and he still didn't have an idea for his project. He trudged up to Mr. Mason's desk as slowly as he could. Mr. Mason smiled at him. "So, Charles, what's your project about?" he asked.

Charles bit his lip.

"I'm guessing it has something to do with puppies," said Mr. Mason.

Charles sat up. Puppies! He hadn't even thought about that. He remembered Lizzie teaching Roxy her new trick the night before. "I wonder . . ." he began slowly, "I wonder if it's really true that using better treats helps dogs learn faster."

Mr. Mason raised his eyebrows, looking confused.

"My aunt Amanda always says it does," Charles explained. "When she's training dogs, she uses stuff like roast beef, or cheddar cheese, instead of regular dog biscuits. But I wonder . . . is it really true that dogs learn faster with those treats? I can do some experiments to find out." His mind was racing. This could be really fun. Sammy could help him, since he had plenty of time while his mold was growing. They could teach Roxy and Buddy all kinds of new tricks, and the people who came to the science fair would learn something about dog training.

Mr. Mason leaned back in his chair, made his fingers into a little tent under his chin, and thought for a moment. Then he sat back up, smiling. "I like it," he said. "Great idea, Charles."

Charles let out a sigh of relief.

"Now all you have to do is design your experiment scientifically," Mr. Mason added.

CHAPTER SEVEN

"Okay, do we have everything we need for our big experiment?" Charles asked Sammy the next day. They were in Charles's backyard, letting Buddy and Roxy roam around before their big training session. Buddy seemed to understand that Roxy was not up for a game of "chase me and I'll chase you." Both dogs wandered around, sniffing things, while the boys got ready. Roxy's leg was still wrapped in purple, but she was healing fast. She was hardly even limping now, and she could even go up and down the stairs by herself.

Charles held a clipboard in his hand, and now he went down the list he'd made the night before, checking items off with a red pen. "Cheddar cheese bites?"

"Check," said Sammy.

"Hot dog slices?" Charles asked.

"Check," said Sammy.

"Regular old brown biscuits?" Charles asked.

Sammy laughed. "Got 'em," he said, holding up the box and shaking it to make the biscuits rattle. "They may be boring, but every dog I know loves them. I'm guessing that your hypothesis will not be correct."

Mr. Mason had talked the day before about hypotheses—good guesses that scientists made about the answers to their "I wonder" questions. Often, experiments were designed to prove a hypothesis. Charles's hypothesis was that Aunt Amanda was right about dogs learning faster with good treats. Aunt Amanda was usually right about anything to do with dogs.

"We'll see," said Charles. He was pretty sure that Buddy would learn just about any trick faster if a piece of cheddar cheese was involved. Buddy always crunched up any dog biscuits that came his way, but he didn't always seem so excited about them. Charles couldn't blame him. Even the ones with fancy ingredients like blueberries or wild-caught Alaskan salmon didn't look or smell very interesting.

"Anyway, let's finish our checklist of stuff we need for our experiment." Charles scanned the paper on his clipboard. He had figured out that the best way to make his experiment scientific was to measure his results and keep track of them. It wasn't so hard, after all. "Stopwatch? Pen? Clipboard?"

"Yup," said Sammy, holding up the stopwatch hanging around his neck. "And yup and yup," he added, pointing to Charles's clipboard and pen.

"And, of course, the most important part of our research project," Charles said, raising his voice as he knelt down and threw his arms open. "Puppies!"

At that, Buddy and Roxy trotted toward them. The two puppies jumped into the boys' arms. Charles nuzzled the top of Roxy's head while Sammy petted Buddy.

"Who's a good girl?" Charles asked as Roxy wriggled happily and licked his cheek. Her funny, furry face tickled Charles.

Me! I'm the best girl!

After a few more hugs, Charles put Roxy down and picked up his clipboard. "Okay, let's get to work," he said. He had decided to teach Roxy and Buddy how to pick something up and then drop it again, into his hand—sort of like fetch, but without all the running. For a moment, Charles wished Lizzie was there, since she was such a good dog trainer. But this was something he wanted to do on his own. It was just as well that Lizzie had decided to go to Caring Paws to check on Roxy's mom and siblings.

"Doesn't Buddy already know how to fetch?" Sammy asked.

"Sort of," said Charles. "He's great at running after something you throw, but not so great at bringing it back or giving it to you. Sometimes I practically have to wrestle with him to get the ball back."

"Or the octopus," said Sammy, holding up the stuffed toy they had decided to use for training. The eight bright purple legs dangled temptingly, and Buddy made a little leap at the toy.

"Uh-uh, Buddy," said Charles. "Sit." He handed the clipboard to Sammy.

"Okay, get ready with the stopwatch," he said. "Let's see how long it takes to train Buddy to do this."

He put the toy on the ground. "Take it," he said. Buddy pounced on the octopus, tail wagging. "Good b—" Charles began, but before he could finish getting the words out, Roxy pounced, too.

The puppies began to play tug-of-war with the toy, wagging their tails as they growled happily, each tugging one purple leg while the octopus head dangled between them. They dug in their back feet and pulled as hard as they could. Buddy was bigger, but feisty little Roxy wouldn't give up. She tugged and tugged, and Buddy pulled back. The toy's squeaker squealed louder and louder.

"Hey! No! C'mon, Roxy, you're going to hurt your leg," said Charles, but he was laughing too hard to sound serious. He rescued the toy, pulling it away from both puppies. "Let's try this again," he said. This time he picked Roxy up and held her as he started over, dropping the octopus at Buddy's feet. "Take it," he said. This was the easy part. Buddy pounced. Before his puppy could start shaking the toy or run off with it, Charles pulled out a treat—the boring brown kind. "Okay, start the timer," he said to Sammy. Then he gave the more difficult command to Buddy. "Drop it," he said, holding out the biscuit, as if to trade it for the toy.

Buddy sniffed at the biscuit, without letting the octopus fall from his jaws. Then he ran off, shaking the octopus happily. Charles laughed again. "He seems more interested in the toy than in the biscuit," he said.

"Should I stop the timer?" Sammy asked. He held up the ticking stopwatch.

"I guess so," said Charles. "Then let's try again with the special treat." Still holding Roxy, he ran after Buddy and managed to get the toy back from him. This time, before he dropped the octopus, he reached into his pocket and pulled a nugget of cheese out of a plastic bag. Buddy sniffed the air, and his ears perked up. "I have a feeling he'll drop the toy for this treat," said Charles, smiling down at his adorable puppy.

He put the octopus down. "Take it," he said quickly, before Buddy could grab it. As Lizzie said, some tricks were just natural dog behavior that you put a command to. "Good boy," Charles said. "Now, drop it." He held out his hand with the treat in it, and Buddy immediately let the toy drop to the ground so he could grab the hunk of cheese and gobble it down.

"Did you see that?" he asked Sammy. "Maybe my hypothesis isn't so bad after all. I think Aunt

Amanda is right. Good treats are the way to go when you're training a dog."

"Maybe," said Sammy. "There's only one problem. I—um—forgot to start the stopwatch." He held up his hands. "Oops."

Charles smacked his forehead. Mr. Mason always said that science wasn't easy. Charles was beginning to see why.

By the end of the session, Roxy and Buddy both knew how to pick up the toy and drop it quickly when Charles gave the commands. The boring biscuits had been put aside, and the cheese and hot dogs were just about gone by the time Lizzie arrived home.

"How's it going?" she asked.

"Great," said Charles. "I think my hypothesis is correct. All I need now is a few more dogs to test it on. Are Roxy's mom and brothers still at Caring Paws?"

Lizzie shook her head. "No, they—" But before she could say more, Charles heard the phone ringing in the kitchen. "Ha!" Lizzie laughed. "I have a feeling this call might be just what you're looking for."

CHAPTER EIGHT

"That was the people who took Roxy's mom and brothers," Mom said after she'd talked on the phone for a while. "They are going to foster them. Lizzie left our phone number with Ms. Dobbins, in case they wanted to get together with us so Roxy could visit with her family. I invited them over."

After dinner, the doorbell rang. "Oh! It's you!" said Charles when he opened the door.

The boy on the porch raised his eyebrows.

"I mean, I recognize you from the science fair," said Charles as he opened the door wider. "You made the robot, right?"

The boy smiled. "That's right." He stuck out his hand, the one that wasn't cradling a puppy. "I'm Derek."

Charles nodded. "I'm Charles. I met your mom at LazerQuest," he said. "She's really cool."

The man behind Derek smiled. "Yes, she is," he agreed. He was holding the other puppy in one hand and a leash in the other. At the end of the leash was Roxy's mom. Her ears were up, and she was staring at something behind Charles.

Charles turned to see Roxy trotting toward them. Her ears were also up, and her eyes sparkled.

Mom! Wow, what are you doing here?

The puppy and her mom touched noses. Their tails wagged madly as they sniffed each other happily. Then Roxy put her paws up on Derek's knee, sniffing at the puppy he held.

Hi, brother! It's great to see you.

"Charles, are you going to invite our company inside?" Mom asked, coming up behind him. She smiled at Derek's dad as she waved them in. "I'm Betsy Peterson."

"Franklin Watts," he said, sticking his hand out for a shake. "Great to meet you."

Derek's dad was big and muscular, with a shaved head and a cool beard. Once he was inside, he squatted to let the puppy down. "There you go, little man," he said. "Check out your sister." He stood back up. "Thanks for having us over," he said. "It's great to get them all together. Also, Ms. Dobbins said you'd be able to give us some tips on fostering pups."

"We'd be happy to," said Mom. "Would you like some cake? I was helping to test recipes today, and I brought home more than we can eat." She explained that she was a newspaper reporter. "My friend Jim writes the cooking column, and this week he's featuring chocolate cake."

"My favorite," said Franklin, smiling. He and Derek followed Mom into the kitchen and joined the Petersons around the table. While Mom cut the cake and passed it around, Franklin explained that he and Derek had just moved into a larger home with an attached barn so that they'd be able to foster more animals. "I'm a wild-life biologist," he told them, "and Derek and I both love animals. We've taken care of every kind of critter you can think of, and then some. Iguanas, monkeys, a baby raccoon—you name it. Not too many puppies, though." He smiled down at the puppies playing under the table. Their mom lay nearby, watching closely. "We're learning fast, with these two scamps."

"We already taught them to sit," Derek reported. "And the one with more brown in his coat already knows how to shake, too."

"Wait till you see what we taught Roxy," said Charles. He told Derek and his dad about his science project.

"That's so cool. Do you have more cheese? Let's go test Roxy's brothers!" said Derek, gulping down the last bite of his cake.

Charles called Sammy, who came back over to help with the timer and record keeping. After he'd had three pieces of cake, Sammy was ready. With Buddy and Roxy showing off their new skills, Roxy's brothers learned fast. Soon, all four puppies knew how to take the ball and drop it.

The next day at Sharing Circle, Charles was full of news about how smart Roxy was and how quickly she and her brothers had learned their new tricks. He also told the class about meeting Derek and his dad. "First I wasn't sure about having another foster family around," he admitted. "But they're great. We can help them learn about fostering puppies. And maybe I'll get to help sometime when they're fostering some other kind of animal, like a skunk or a fawn."

"You'll learn a lot from Franklin," said Mr. Mason. "He knows so much about animals. But you're still fostering Roxy, though, right?" he asked. He looked a little worried.

"Yup," said Charles. "She's used to us now, so we'll keep her until we find her the right home. I'm sure somebody will want to adopt her soon." The thought made him sad, but he wanted what was best for Roxy.

When it was time for recess, Mr. Mason asked Charles to stay in the classroom for a moment. "I have a big favor to ask you," he said.

Charles was surprised. What could he do for Mr. Mason? "Okay," he said. "What is it?"

"It has to do with Roxy," said Mr. Mason. "Maybe I could come to your house tonight so I can see her trick in person, and we can talk with your parents about whether you and Roxy can help me."

CHAPTER NINE

"Honey, Derek's here with the puppies!" Mom called from the deck. It was a few days after Mr. Mason had visited, and Charles and Roxy were out in the backyard waiting for Derek to come by for puppy playtime. While they waited, Charles had been working hard on the little pup's training.

Roxy pricked up her ears. She sniffed the air and let out three little barks.

My family! Yay!!

Charles scooped Roxy up and gave her a hug. "Good job on the training today," he said.

"Mr. Mason is going to be really happy when he sees what you can do." Then he pretended to zip his lips. "But remember, it's a secret. We can't tell anybody, and that includes Derek and your brothers."

Roxy looked up at him with her sparkling brown eyes. He could have sworn that she gave him a wink.

It's our secret. I won't tell a soul.

"Hey, man, how's it going?" Derek asked as he came down the back stairs into the yard, carrying both of Roxy's brothers. "How's Roxy? I see that the purple tape is gone. Is her leg all better?"

Charles nodded. "We went to see Dr. Gibson yesterday, and she said Roxy's healing has been amazing. She's got the green light to do whatever she wants."

"Yesss!" said Derek. "I know two puppies who are going to be very happy to hear that." He grinned at Charles as he let the puppies down onto the grass. "Go play, little dudes."

Charles put Roxy down, and she and her brothers tumbled and wrestled, letting out tiny yips and play growls as they rolled around in the grass. Derek laughed as he watched Roxy pounce on her brothers. "She's a little tiger, isn't she?" he asked.

"She's so smart, too," said Charles. "I mean, of course her brothers are smart. But I think Roxy's the smartest."

"Could be," said Derek. "Maybe we'll have to give them one of those doggy IQ tests sometime. Remember that girl at the science fair who showed how to measure how smart dogs are?"

"That was a good exhibit, but yours was the best," said Charles. "How did you make that robot, anyway?"

Derek laughed. "It took a long time," he said. "Like, months of work. But it was fun. How's your project coming along? Your science fair is tomorrow night, isn't it?"

"Yup," said Charles. "But I'm almost ready. Want to see the poster I made for my display?"

"Definitely," said Derek. "I'll watch the pups while you get it."

Charles ran inside and came back out with a large piece of white poster board. On it he had drawn two giant stopwatch faces, with the hands in red and the numbers in black. One showed that thirteen seconds had gone by, and the other showed thirty-seven seconds. "I haven't finished it yet, but this shows the average time for a puppy to learn a trick with the extra-good treats," Charles said, pointing to the thirteen-second clock. "And that one shows the average time with plain biscuits."

"Great!" said Derek. "I like your presentation. With a science fair, sometimes it's all about the poster."

"I'm bringing Roxy, too," said Charles. "I think she'll add a lot to my display. She can do the tricks she's learned, and everybody will love her. Maybe somebody will even decide to adopt her!" He was dying to tell Derek the other reason he was bringing Roxy, but he couldn't. That was between him and Mr. Mason.

"Your presentation is going to be the best one in the whole second grade," said Derek. "I can't wait to see it."

"You're coming?" Charles asked.

"Sure," said Derek. "I mean, my mom and I will be there, you know, because she and Mr. Mason—" He grinned. "I mean, your teacher is my mom's boyfriend. How weird is that?"

"Kind of weird," said Charles. "But I like your mom a lot."

"And I like Mr. Mason a lot, too," said Derek. "He's really cool, for an older dude."

Charles couldn't help smiling. "Yeah, he's cool," he said. Again, he wished he could tell Derek the big secret Mr. Mason shared with him, but he couldn't. He just couldn't. He picked up a tennis ball and called the puppies over. "Come on, Roxy! Come on, puppies," he said, holding up the ball. "Let's play a little fetch!" He tossed the ball, and the puppies scrambled after it, falling over their own feet. "Have you named the puppies yet?" he asked Derek.

Derek shook his head. "No, my dad and I are just calling them both Little Man. My mom's the one who is good at naming, and she hasn't met them yet. Anyway, we're only fostering them. We won't be keeping them for long." He looked wistful as he watched the puppies play.

"That's the hardest part of fostering," Charles said. "When you have to say good-bye to the puppies."

Derek nodded. Then he brightened. "But I think I talked my dad into adopting their mom! We even named her. We've been calling her Ruby. She's an amazing dog. I think that's where Roxy got her feistiness from."

Charles gave Derek a high five. "When you have your own dog, it's a lot easier to say good-bye to the foster puppies," he said. "That's what we found out when we adopted Buddy." Charles smiled at Derek. He had a feeling that Ruby was going to be very happy with this boy and his dad.

CHAPTER TEN

Charles felt a little tingle as his dad pulled into the school parking lot. The big sign with changeable letters said SCIENCE FAIR TONIGHT! He clutched his rolled-up poster tightly, wondering for the tenth time if he should have made the lettering even bigger, or if he should have added a chart or a graph.

Dad met his eyes in the rearview mirror. "Nothing to be nervous about," he said, as if he was reading Charles's mind. "Your project is terrific, and everybody's going to love Roxy."

Charles smiled down at the puppy in his lap. Dad was right about one thing. Roxy was one of

71

the most loveable puppies they had ever fostered. Now that her leg was better, she was a little spitfire, tearing around the house and getting into everything. Still, no matter what kind of trouble she got into, Charles could never be mad at her.

"You're just too cute," said Charles, ruffling her fur. "Who's the cutest?"

Roxy looked up at him, cocked her head, and wagged her tiny tail.

Me! I know I am! But I love hearing it.

Charles smiled at Roxy, but he still felt nervous. The project was not the only thing Charles was worried about tonight. There was something much more important on his mind. Soon, everyone would know, and he wouldn't have to keep Mr. Mason's secret any longer—but until then,

Charles couldn't stop wondering how it would all turn out. He was hoping for the best, but anything could happen.

"Here we go," said Dad, pulling into a parking spot. He held Roxy while Charles got out of the van, and they walked to the main entrance, Charles carrying his poster. As soon as he opened the big door, Charles spotted Mr. Mason waiting just inside.

"Dad, can you take Roxy and my poster over to the hallway near room 2B?" he asked. "I need to check with Mr. Mason about our plan."

"Of course," said Dad, winking at Charles. "I know this is a big night for Mr. Mason." He pretended to zip his lips. "Don't worry, I won't spill the beans."

Charles handed his poster to Dad. Then he joined Mr. Mason by the drinking fountain. His

73

teacher looked nervous. He wiped some sweat off his forehead with a folded-up handkerchief as he greeted Charles.

"Are we all set?" he asked. "Roxy knows what to do?" He took a deep breath. "I sure wish we'd had more time to practice together."

"It'll be fine," said Charles. "Just remember the cues. 'Take it' for her to pick it up, and 'drop it' for letting it go."

Mr. Mason nodded. "Got it," he said. He reached into his pocket and pulled out a small blue velvet bag with a gold ribbon drawstring. "Here it is!"

"Wow, pretty," said Charles. He felt sorry for Mr. Mason, who already had more little beads of sweat on his forehead. "Don't worry. It's all going to go great," he said, patting Mr. Mason's arm as he put the bag back into his pocket.

Mr. Mason smiled. "Thanks. Now get going!

You only have a few minutes left to set up your display."

Charles headed down the hall and found Sammy outside their classroom. He and Dad were already taping up Charles's poster near the table where Sammy had displayed his mold projects.

"These are fantastic," said Charles, looking over the plastic bags full of weird and colorful molds growing on different foods. Sammy had made hilarious name tags for each one.

"I know," said Sammy. "Best project ever. I bet I win an award."

Once Charles had put his poster up, there wasn't much to do but wait. Charles felt in his pocket for the special treats—string cheese and bacon-flavored jerky—he had brought for Roxy. He called Roxy over and showed Sammy how good she had gotten at her fetch trick.

"Take it," he said, pointing to the octopus toy he had brought along. Roxy scampered over and grabbed the toy in her tiny jaws, shaking it happily. "Good girl," said Charles. He pointed to Sammy. "Now go to Sammy and drop it." She pranced over to Sammy and plopped the octopus right into his hand. "Good girl!" Charles said again. "Perfect!" He gave her a tiny piece of jerky. She was such a smarty. It had not been hard at all to do what Mr. Mason had asked—teach Roxy to take the toy to a nearby person. All he had to do was point and say the commands.

What could go wrong?

Charles tried not to think about it. Instead, he carried Roxy in his arms while he examined Sammy's molds carefully, reading the name tags Sammy had made for each one.

Charles laughed. The signs were hilarious, if not exactly scientific. Like, "Hi, I'm Cladosporium bread mold. Please don't eat me unless you want to get really sick!" That was Sammy for you. He couldn't resist a joke.

Then Charles felt a tap on his shoulder. He spun around to see Mr. Mason, with Janice and Derek.

"Oh!" said Janice. "She's the cutest!"

At the word "cutest," Roxy tilted her head and looked at Janice, her eyes sparkling.

Exactly! That's me! I think you and I are going to get along great.

Janice looked like she was about to faint from the cuteness. Then Mr. Mason cleared his throat. "I knew you'd love her," he said. "And I know how long you've wanted a dog. So I have a question for you. What would you think about adopting Roxy?"

Janice bit her lip. "I'd love to, but I've told you. As a single mom—"

Mr. Mason pulled the blue velvet bag out of his pocket. He looked at Roxy. "Take it," he said, holding it out for the little pup to see.

Roxy trotted right over and took the bag gently in her teeth, carrying it by its gold satin ribbon. Then Mr. Mason pointed at Janice, and Roxy started to head her way. "Give it to Janice," he said.

Roxy stopped in her tracks and looked back at him.

Hmmm, I don't know that one. Can you explain what you want?

"Drop it," Charles whispered.

Immediately, Roxy ran up to Janice and dropped the bag into her outstretched hand. "Oh!" said Janice, picking up Roxy and cradling her in her arms. "What a good girl." She was so busy kissing the top of Roxy's head that she ignored the bag in her hand.

"Open it!" called Charles. He couldn't stand the suspense a moment longer.

Janice looked down at the bag. Holding Roxy carefully, she fumbled with the satin drawstring and untied the bow. She opened the bag and pulled out a small blue box. Then she looked up at Mr. Mason, and a smile lit up her face.

Mr. Mason looked back at Janice, blushing and smiling.

"Open it!" Charles yelled again. This time, he was joined by Derek, Sammy, and a bunch of other kids and parents who had gathered around.

Janice flipped the box open, still clutching Roxy. Charles saw the sparkle of the diamond ring Mr. Mason had told him was inside.

"Janice," said Mr. Mason as he knelt down on one knee. "Will you marry me? I want you and me and Derek and Roxy to be a family together."

Now Janice was crying fat tears that slid down her cheeks. But she was smiling, too. She looked over at Derek, who gave her two thumbs up. "Yes," she said, turning back to Mr. Mason. "Yes, of course." She handed Roxy to Charles and ran to Mr. Mason for a hug and a kiss that made everybody hoot and break into cheers and applause.

Derek grinned at Charles from across the crowd. Charles grinned back. It had worked! Even though Mr. Mason had given the wrong cue, Roxy knew just what to do. The smart little pup had known exactly how to prove that she belonged as part of this new family. Charles was going to be sorry to see Roxy go, but he knew she would be in good hands. Plus, he had a feeling that his family and Derek's were going to be friends, which meant he would be seeing a lot more of Roxy. Suddenly, Charles didn't care whether his science project won a prize or not. After all, how could this night be any more perfect?

PUPPY TIPS

What should you do if you find a sick or injured puppy or dog? First of all, tell an adult. Not all injured dogs should be moved. If you have a blanket or a sweater handy, you can put that over the dog to keep him warm and cozy while you wait for help. You can stay with the dog and help to keep him calm by stroking him gently or speaking in a quiet voice—but only if the dog seems comfortable with that. Even gentle dogs may behave in a fearful or angry way when they are hurt. A grown-up can help you take the dog to a vet's office or a pet emergency care center. If you would like to learn more about pet first aid, you might be able to find a class at your local animal shelter.

Dear Reader,

It can be so scary when your dog is sick or injured. I've been through some tough experiences with my dogs over the years. Django once ate something that made him very, very sick — so sick that he had to stay overnight at the vet's! Zipper cut his leg badly on the sharp edge of my ski, and had to have stitches. And, long ago, my dog Jack actually broke his tail! He had to have it wrapped just like Roxy's leg, and he looked very silly. I am thankful to have had great vets to take my dogs to, and with good care they all healed and went back to their happy lives.

Yours from the Puppy Place,

Ellen Miles

THE PUPPY PLACE

DON'T MISS THE
NEXT PUPPY PLACE
ADVENTURE!

Here's a peek at KODIAK

"Wow, I forgot how beautiful it is up here," said Kamala. "Look at the way these huge old trees arch over the road. And the fall colors are amazing."

In the back seat, Lizzie Peterson and her best friend Maria Santiago grinned at each other. "Amazing," echoed Lizzie.

They were on their way to the Santiagos' cabin in the country. Lizzie had been there many times before, but always with Maria's parents. This time, they were with Maria's cousin Kamala. She was a grownup, but just barely—she was twenty-two and had just finished college. Going to the cabin with Kamala felt like a big adventure, and Lizzie was excited.

"When is the last time you were up here?" Maria asked her cousin.

"It has to be, like, eight years ago!" Kamala answered. "I remember I had this new camera I'd gotten for my birthday. I must have taken a thousand pictures. I probably still have some of them. You were the cutest thing, in your little pink overalls. You were barely walking then."

Maria laughed. "I remember my pink overalls but I don't remember that trip."

"You sure have grown up a lot since then," said Kamala. "I really appreciate you and Lizzie coming up here with me to help me get settled in."

Kamala was planning to stay at the cabin for a few weeks. She'd asked Maria's parents if she could spend some time there while she figured out what she wanted to do next in her life. After this weekend she would drive Lizzie and Maria home, then go back up and be on her own at the cabin.

"I still can't believe my parents let me come," said Lizzie. "Maybe my mom just wanted me out of her hair for a while."

"What?" Kamala asked. She met Lizzie's eyes in the rearview mirror. "Why?"

Lizzie shrugged. "She says I've been acting like Eeyore lately, whining and complaining about everything."

"And—have you?" Kamala asked.

"Well, maybe a little," Lizzie said. She didn't know exactly why she'd been feeling so cranky lately, but for some reason it was easier to admit it to Kamala than to her mom.

Kamala laughed. "Hopefully this trip will help you break that habit," she said. "I might have even some ideas that could help."

Kamala turned off the tree-lined highway and onto a narrow, bumpy dirt road. "Almost there!" she said. "We'll have a lot to do when we arrive: unload the car, get firewood, start a fire, get dinner going, set the table . . ."

At home, Lizzie would have groaned if she'd heard a list of chores like that. But the cabin was different. She could hardly wait to get there and get to work. There was something really special about the Santiagos' cozy little cabin in the woods.

The only thing missing on this trip was a dog. Usually Simba would be along. He was Mrs. Santiago's guide dog, a big yellow lab. Maria's mom was blind and she usually had Simba at her side. He was a total sweetheart, and Lizzie loved it when Mrs. Santiago told her it was okay to pet and cuddle him a bit when he was off duty. But since Maria's mom wasn't coming this weekend, that also meant Simba wasn't going to be there.

Lizzie would have liked to bring her puppy, Buddy, but that idea had been vetoed by everyone else in the family. The Petersons were all in love with Buddy. Lizzie could just imagine the scene at home: her two younger brothers, Charles and the Bean, would be squabbling over whose room Buddy would sleep in that night. Mom would be slipping him extra treats "just because," even though Lizzie always told her that he should have to earn them by doing tricks. And Dad would be ruffling his ears and asking him over and over if he was a good boy. Buddy sure did get plenty of attention at the Petersons' house!

"Buddy face," said Maria, poking Lizzie in the ribs.

"What's that?" asked Kamala, glancing into the rearview mirror.

Lizzie and Maria giggled. "It's just the face Lizzie makes when she's thinking about her puppy—or really about any dog," explained Maria. "Which is basically all the time," she added, with another giggle. Maria knew that Lizzie was totally dog crazy. She'd spent plenty of time in Lizzie's room, which was decorated in Everything Dog. She knew that Lizzie had dog-themed socks, pajamas, and even underpants, and that Lizzie collected dog books, dog figurines, and of course every color and breed of dog stuffie.

"Lizzie's family fosters puppies," Maria told her cousin. "They've taken care of so many adorable puppies who needed help. They find the best homes for every one of them! Their puppy Buddy was a foster puppy at first, but now he's their forever dog."

ABOUT THE AUTHOR

Ellen Miles loves dogs, which is why she has a great time writing the Puppy Place books. And guess what? She loves cats, too! (In fact, her very first pet was a beautiful tortoiseshell cat named Jenny.) That's why she came up with the Kitty Corner series. Ellen lives in Vermont and loves to be outdoors with her dog, Zipper, every day, walking, biking, skiing, or swimming, depending on the season. She also loves to read, cook, explore her beautiful state, play with dogs, and hang out with friends and family.

Visit Ellen at ellenmiles.net.